God, I Need to Talk to You about BEDTIME

Written by Susan K. Leigh
Pictures by Bill Clark

CONCORDIA PUBLISHING HOUSE • SAINT LOUIS

Dear God,
    I'm supposed to be getting **ready for bed**. I brushed my teeth. I turned down my covers. And Dad read my favorite book to me. Twice.

Dad kissed me goodnight, and Mom tucked me in. They said my prayers with me. Mom let me have one more drink of water. But I'm **not sleepy!**

Better is a handful of quietness than two hands full of toil and a striving after wind.
Ecclesiastes 4:6

I'd rather watch a movie or play a game. I'd rather read another book or play with my toys.

I **don't** want to go to bed yet.

But Mom and Dad said it's my **bedtime**. They said if I don't get enough sleep, I'll be cranky.

Mom said **everybody** needs to sleep. Grownups get to stay up longer, but they still have a regular bedtime. Kids need more sleep because we're growing all the time and that takes a lot of energy.

When you lie down, your sleep will be sweet.

Proverbs 3:24

Dad said that You made day and night so we would have time to work and **time to rest**. We need to rest so we can be strong and healthy. Not cranky.

Then Dad said that even **You rested**.
I hadn't thought of that before.

God rested from all His work that He had done in creation.

Genesis 2:3

Mom said **Jesus rested** too. Like the time He was in the boat on the sea and woke up so He could calm the storm.

He awoke and rebuked the wind and
the raging waves, and they ceased,
and there was a calm.

Luke 14:22

So, God, now I understand about getting rest and how You planned it that way. I guess I'm sleepy after all. **Good night**, God. I love You! Amen.